Mon Amour

Cat Voleur

Copyright © 2024 by Cat Voleur

All rights reserved.

No part of this publication may be reproduced, distributed, or transmitted in any form or by any means, including photocopying, recording, or other electronic or mechanical methods, without the prior written permission of the publisher, except as permitted by U.S. copyright law.

The story, all names, characters, and incidents portrayed in this production are fictitious. No identification with actual persons (living or deceased), places, buildings, and products is intended or should be inferred.

Book Cover by Ruth Anna Evans

Contents

Dedication	IV
Mon Amour	1
Acknowledgements	77
Content Warnings	79
Also By	80

For John and Amanda,

My perpetual valentines

Mon Amour

> Would you forgive me if I'd done something bad, mon amour?

> Something bad?

> Yes

> How bad?

> Unforgivable

> You want me to forgive the unforgivable?

> For me?

> You know I'd do anything for you, mon amour.

Do you promise?

> Well of course.

Say it

> Say what?

Say you promise

> Can I know what you did first?

No

> Well what if it's something truly terrible?

It is

> I see.

> And you won't tell ?

No. Not until you promise

> Hm.

Maybe not even then

Well, since you won't tell me until I promise, maybe you can promise me something as well?

Anything

A picture?

Oh

Is that so wrong?

You know how I feel about pictures

I know.

That's why it's a punishment.

Unless you're teasing me.

Maybe what you did isn't so bad after all?

If that were the case, you could just tell me. No need for a picture.

I'd never tease you

Not about this

I was going to say…

It truly is worse than you're expecting

Do you think you deserve a punishment then?

I do

Then you'll send a picture?

Why do you want a picture of me so much?

You're beautiful.

You don't know that though

I can tell.

No one can really tell

I could be a man

I could be a child

Ginny, what the hell?

> That's sick
>
> Don't even joke about that

Would that bother you?

> If you were a fucking kid?

Yes

> Yes that would bother me.
>
> I could go to jail

It's not illegal here

> It is here!
>
> What the fuck?

Only if I told

> Stop it
>
> Fuck.

> Fuck. Is that why you don't want to send a picture?
>
> You told me you were an adult.
>
> Jesus fucking christ
>
> Tell me you're at least 18
>
> Ginny!

I'm 18

A little older actually

> What the fuck?
>
> You scared the shit out of me

Sorry

I was just curious

> Curious?

You said you knew that I was beautiful

I wanted to see how sure you were

> Well don't do that again.

> Don't ever fucking joke about that.

I won't

> It wasn't funny.

Sorry

> Is that the bad thing you did? Are you catfishing me? Are you a man?

I'm not a man

> But?

But I do have secrets

> Secrets you think I'll be angry about?

Exactly.

> But you won't tell me?

Not until you promise

> And you won't take the punishment?

> I never said that

>> You haven't sent a picture.

> After

> Tell me first

> What do you think I look like?

>> I don't know.

> You said you knew

>> I didn't mean I knew what you looked like, only that I can tell you're beautiful

> Tell me what that means to you

>> It could mean a lot of things

> It could

> But it doesn't

>> Looks don't matter to me.

> Looks matter to everyone

> Not to me.

> I'm sure you have a type?

> Do you?

> Have a type, I mean?

> Maybe

> Tell me.

> I asked first, mon amour

> I suppose

> If I had to choose

> Of all the many beautiful kinds of women

> I would say that I like redheads

> Keep going

> Pale, slender redheads.

> With red lips?

> Yes. Dark red.

And green eyes?

Beautiful.

How do you feel about tattoos?

Do you have tattoos?

Would that bother you?

No.

I like tattoos.

I like that level of commitment to something.

The willingness to endure.

For beauty.

And pain

Yes. That too.

Would it surprise you if I had them?

Very little would surprise me about you.

> Especially after that stunt you pulled.

Sorry

> If you were really sorry…

A picture?

> Just one.

You seem really set on this tonight

> I just want to see you.
>
> Just once.
>
> It will be another year at least before I can get the time off to visit you.
>
> And we've been talking for so long.
>
> I just want to feel closer to you.
>
> Please?

I just don't know that I feel comfortable with it

> Why?

I don't know

Are you afraid I might do something with it?

You might

Or you could get hacked

You might think I'm ugly

Or get tired of me.

Okay.

Well you know I'd never do anything with them. And even if I did, you have those pictures of me.

I would definitely know if I got hacked, but I won't save the picture if you want. I know you'll be beautiful and I'll be even less tired of you.

This will bring us closer.

Can I tell you something that scares me?

About the picture?

Yes

> Of course.

> You can tell me anything.

I'm afraid it will change things between us

Once you've seen me

> Why would you think that?

Fear isn't always rational

What we have is just so special

> But don't you think it could be more special?

Maybe

> Please?

I'll send you one picture

> Thank you.

But not now

> When?

Tonight

If you stay long enough

And if you promise

And if you can keep that promise

Thank you.

I promise, mon amour.

Say the whole thing.

Say that you promise to forgive me.

I promise to forgive you.

Good

So what did you do?

Not yet

I want you to tell me first

Tell you what?

A secret

> A secret?

Yes

> You know I don't keep secrets from you.

None?

> None.
>
> I'm an open book.

So you're saying you would tell me anything?

> Anything.

Tell me something about you, then

Something I don't know yet

> You know me so well.

I'm sure I don't know everything

> Well…

It would make me feel better

> Is that so?

Yes

It would make me feel like I could trust you

> You don't trust me?

Of course I trust you

But can I TRUST you?

To be open

And honest

And bad?

> You want me to be bad?

I think you already are

> Oh?

I think we all are

Everyone

Everyone is a little bad sometimes

> Maybe you're right.

So tell me something a little bad about yourself

> Maybe you could start?

> Help me out by asking me something?

Alright

Let me think for a minute

> Take your time.

Okay, I have one

> May I hear it?

Yes

But you have to answer honestly

> Always

Okay

What is the worst thing you ever did on purpose?

> On purpose?

Yeah

What's the worst thing you ever did that you MEANT to do?

> What a strange question.

Is it?

> I half expected the first part. The worst thing I ever did. But not the on purpose bit.

I think we all do bad things accidentally sometimes

Sometimes we probably don't even know the worst thing we've ever done to someone else.

It's hard to know what the consequences of our actions are

> You're probably right about that.

> The bad thing YOU did.

> Was it on purpose?

Yes

> And you're still planning on telling me?

Yes

> I guess I'd better tell you then

Yes

> Well, here it goes.

I'm ready

> I locked my little brother in the shed.

That doesn't sound so terrible

> It was worse than it sounds.

Tell me

> It was cold, for one.
>
> And I left him out there overnight.

How old were you?

> 12

> He was only 9

Why did you do it?

> Well, it just started that I wanted to scare him. There was this old tool shed out in the woods.

> We weren't really supposed to be out there. Mom was always worried it would cave in and one of us would get hurt.

But you played out there anyway?

> All the time.

> And one day I just closed the door behind him. It was just supposed to be a joke. A prank. I was going to scare him and then let him out.

So what happened?

> He got scared.

> He got REALLY scared.

> He started screaming and crying and he said he was going to tell our mom.

So you kept him in there?

Exactly.

I told him I was going to let him out when he calmed down.

And did you?

I would have.

He said something was crawling on him, and it must have scared him pretty bad because he just. Kept. Screaming.

So you stayed?

Oh no.

I would have gotten in big trouble.

What did you do instead?

I went home. Without him.

I snuck in through the window and so when it was time for dinner I just came out of my room. Said I thought he was playing with his toys alone.

How did that work?

> Really well at first.

> Too well.

> Mom was livid.

> I guess he had been asking to go see a movie with one of his friends, and dad had said no.

> I didn't know that.

> When he turned up missing, that's where they thought he'd gone.

Did he do that sort of thing often? Sneak out?

At 9?

> Well no.

> But they didn't tell him no very often.

> He was the baby.

> He was always getting his way about everything.

> And then they finally told him no.

> That it wouldn't be fair to me if I didn't get to go too, even though they weren't my friends.

> The first time telling him no, and then he went missing while his friends were all at the movies.

So you let your mom be mad at him?

> I did.

> Can I tell you something terrible?

Of course

> It was nice

> It was a short dinner, but I was the focus of it.

> That didn't happen to me anymore.

> I hadn't been the focus of anything since I was a toddler.

> I was enjoying myself, until dinner ended and mom starting making phone calls.

Who did she call?

> She got ahold of the friend's mom and suddenly my little brother wasn't misbehaving, he was missing proper.

And you still didn't tell her?

No.

She'd have killed me.

I figured I'd go out and help look and be the hero when I came home with him.

So why didn't you?

Was he still screaming?

I took too long.

I didn't want to go right to him because I thought it would look too suspicious. And I like you said, I thought he might still be screaming. So went out the wrong way and called his name and pretended to look.

But then mom got panicked.

She thought maybe he'd been grabbed, and she was afraid I'd get taken too.

So she made me come inside.

And you went?

Yes.

I thought they'd find him any minute. They'd see how I'd propped the wood up against the door so it wouldn't open. They'd hear him screaming.

And he'd tell them I'd done it and then everything would be over.

What did you do?

There was nothing I could do.

Nothing I could think of anyway.

I knew mom would be paying attention and I'd only get myself in more trouble if I tried to sneak out.

Eventually she came to tuck me in.

She was crying.

I was crying too.

I remember thinking that would probably be the last time she ever tucked me in.

I'd been saying for a year that I was too big for it anyway. But I knew it was different. She'd never WANT to tuck me in again after what I'd done and that hurt.

> I stayed up all night because that hurt so much and there was nothing I could do to make it right.

Did she?

Tuck you in after that I mean?

> All the time.

> She never found out what I did.

Because you let him out?

> Because the shed collapsed.

Oh

I'm sorry

Was he okay?

> No.

> Yes.

> Sort of? Eventually.

Tell me

> He'd been hit on the head pretty hard, and scraped up pretty good.

> He caught pneumonia.

> The doctors said he was very, VERY lucky to be alive.

And he never told on you?

> He said later on he didn't remember anything about that night. He didn't know why he had been out there or how the shed had collapsed.

> My parents believed him.

But you didn't?

> No.

> I guess I didn't.

Why?

> We were never close after that.

> The way he looked at me was different.

> I was a lot nicer to him and he always just kept his distance. I think he was afraid of me, but he never said it out loud and he never told her what I'd done.

What reason did he have to lie for you?

> Maybe he thought I would do it again if he told.

You couldn't have done it again

The shed was gone

> Maybe he thought I'd do something worse.

Would you have?

> No.

Are you sure?

> No.

Thank you

For telling me

Can I tell you something?

> Sure.

> I wasn't sure that counted. I almost called you out for cheating

> Cheating?

> At our game

> You didn't really mean to do all that, after all

> I've never told anyone that story.

> Don't worry

> I've decided to count it

> Good.

> I'm bearing my soul to you here, Ginny.

> Yes

> You are

> But that's not why it counts

> Why then?

> If my honesty isn't good enough for you?

Because my story is the same way

It was one small thing I did on purpose

And then it spiraled out

I MEANT to do the first part

But I didn't know everything that would come after

Or how bad it would be

> So you'd be cheating, too.

Only if I decide that yours is cheating, though

> Right.

Are you mad at me?

> No.

Are you lying?

> I'm not in the mood, Ginny.

> Tell me what you did.

That's not the deal.

> It is.
>
> I promised to forgive you for whatever thing you did.
>
> I told you something personal.
>
> I didn't expect you to fucking rate me on it.
>
> I've held up my end anyway.
>
> So just tell me.

You are angry

> Tell me, or I'm calling it a night. I've got to work tomorrow anyway and it's getting late.

I don't want you to be angry before I even tell you

> Goodnight, Ginny.

Wait

> Don't you want to see your picture?

> You do

> I can see you typing and deleting and typing again

> You're still here

> I know you want to see

>> Ginny, I told you. I'm not in a mood to play anymore.

> Talking about your brother really ruined the evening, huh?

>> It wasn't that.

> What was it?

>> I don't know that I want the picture after all.

> You're scared too, aren't you?

> That I'm not pretty

>> Looks don't matter to me.

> This whole thing is ruined if I'm not pretty

> It's not that.

What, then?

> Maybe we're getting a little too serious.
>
> Maybe seeing a picture will change something.
>
> Maybe talking is better until I can come out there and we can sort it out.

You told me something you'd never told anyone

And now you feel vulnerable?

> I did.

Thank you

For sharing that story with me

Can I tell you something?

> Sure.

That's how I feel sometimes

> In front of the camera

> Why?

> Something bad happened to me once

> And now I always feel like I'm being watched

> It's worse when I'm in front of the camera

> I feel like people can see right through me

> I feel vulnerable all the time

> I'm sorry.

> I wouldn't have asked if I had known that was why.

> It's not a good feeling, is it?

> Being exposed like that

> No.

> I guess it doesn't feel too good.

> I'm sorry I had to do that to you

> to make you understand

I just wanted to trust you a little more.

You don't have to send me a picture tonight.

We can just talk.

I want to

I want to show you what I look like, if you're still interested after we talk

Why?

Because you were vulnerable with me?

Because I always keep my promises?

Because I want you to know that you can be vulnerable with me and I won't go anywhere.

Thank you.

For trusting me.

You have to earn it

I'm really afraid that after I share what I've done you're not going to love me anymore

> I'll always love you.

> What was it you taught me?

Je t'aime toujour.

> That's right.

> Je t'aime toujour.

Can I ask you just one more question before I tell you?

> Yes.

Did you like it?

> Like what?

The power

Of knowing your little brother was scared of you?

> That's a terrible thing to ask.

I know

But did you?

> Sometimes.

Thank you

For being being honest with me.

> Always.

> Now please.

Right

So

The bad thing that I did

I lied to you

> About what?

A lot of things

It's like the shed

I meant to tell you one small lie

But then there were consequences

> What was the small lie?

My name isn't French

What?

Remember the first conversation we ever had?

You asked me if I'd tell you my name, and not just my screen name, but my real name. So that we could feel less anonymous?

I told you it was Genevieve

And you asked if that was English or French

And I said it was French

Because I wanted to sound more interesting

But it's English?

Is that all?

You want to know the craziest part? I don't even know

I don't know if it's English or French or some wild third thing

But weren't you named after your mother?

> Your French mother.

That's what they told me was most likely

I never knew my mother

Or my father

The "father" that I told you about was the father that I had in foster care

> I'm so sorry.

Thank you

> But wait.

Yes?

> If your name isn't French…

C'est vrai

Those would be the consequences.

> How much of what you told me has been made up?

The personal stuff is all true

After a fashion

But the professional things…

Where I work

Where I live

What languages I'm fluent in…

> You don't speak French?

Je ne parle pas français

> What?

> You made it all up?

> It's just gibberish?

Google translate

> How do you survive in Paris?

> You don't.

> You don't live in Paris, do you?

I don't live in Paris.

> I was going to come visit you!

I know.

Je sais

It's one of the reasons I'm coming clean

Are you angry?

> I'm...confused.
>
> Why would you lie about that?

I didn't know we'd get so close

I didn't expect for us to keep talking for so long

I just wanted to be impressive for a night

To be exotic

And captivating

A mystery

> And then we kept talking...

Yes

And the lies got more elaborate

And honestly

I liked them

I liked being an exotic French mystery

It was a lot better than being Little Orphan Ginny from Seattle

I loved being Mon Amour

> Seattle?

And can I tell you something else?

> You're from Seattle?

She felt more real to me than I am

These conversations are the realest thing that I do these days

It was most like my other life was a lie

Does that make sense?

> Ginny.

Being two different people… it's hard though

Especially when you like one of them so much better

I like being her

Ginny

Me

This version of myself

It was like sliding into a second skin and finding out that skin fit me better than my own

Ginny.

Exactly

Ginny

So in a way

It's not like I've lied to you

It's more like I was lying to everyone before you

> Mon amour.

Yes?

> You said you were from Seattle?

Yes

> Where in Seattle?

Downtown

Why?

Are you worried you've seen me somewhere before?

> I don't live in Seattle.

No

But you've been here before

You came here for a business trip

> I don't remember telling you that.

You seem awfully fixated on the city

> It's not too far. If you'd told me, I could have come to see you sooner. A trip to Seattle is easier than a trip to Paris.

I wasn't ready

> Ready?

To meet you

I wasn't me yet

I didn't trust you enough

And I was vulnerable

And I thought you'd be mad

> I'm not mad.

So you'll keep your promise?

> Sure.

You forgive me?

> Yes.

Do you mean it?

> Or are you just saying you do so you can get that picture?

> I mean it.

> I forgive you.

> You seem different

> Colder

> It's just a lot to take in.

> I understand

> Do you want to see that picture now?

> Sure.

> Can I tease you a little bit first?

> I'm not sure I'm in the mood.

> You said it's late there. Are you in bed?

> Yes.

> Maybe it will get me in the mood? If you're in the mood?

> I could tell you what I'm wearing?

>> What are you wearing?

> Lingerie

>> I'd ask you to prove it but… you know. The camera thing.

> It's what I'll be wearing when I take the picture.

>> Really?

> So help me get in the mood?

>> Fuck.

>> Yes.

>> Tell me how.

> What do you like to think about?

> When we talk

>> You

> Me?

> Just you.

And you too, right?

> Oh, I'm there.

Am I doing things to you?

> Yes.

Are you doing things to me?

> Yes.

What am I wearing?

> Lingerie.

What kind?

> One of those little night gowns.

Is it silky?

> Yes.

Is it cream colored?

Sure.

Is it stained?

Are you… saying you're a dirty girl? Who can't even keep her clothes clean? Do you need punished?

Maybe I've already been punished?

Yes.

Maybe I'm already bleeding

Fuck.

In the rain

Ginny.

Hang on.

What?

Does that get you in the mood?

Can we stop for a second?

Is that an order, mon amour?

Yes.

I order you to stop.

Ginny, this is getting weird again.

Are you turned on?

Ginny, I mean it.

Sorry. You didn't use our safe word

We don't have a safe word.

Exactly ;)

No, hang on.

I'm a little uncomfortable.

About the blood?

I thought you'd like getting a little rough with me

In public

> No.
>
> Not the blood.
>
> The other thing.

The rain?

> No.
>
> The silk.
>
> Why is the silk cream colored?

I thought it would be sexy

It shows off all the blood

> Are you messing with me right now?

No

It's what I'm wearing right now

Cream silk

> Okay, can I get serious for a second?

We've already established that you can

> I'm having a tough time after all.
>
> With your secret.

You're breaking your promise?

> No.

I do forgive you, but I have some follow up questions.

> I need help getting my head around it.

Alright

What can I do to help?

> Maybe we can just talk about something else for awhile?
>
> Lay off the kinky stuff until I've adjusted?

Sure

If that's what you want

> I think so.
>
> I'd like to ask you a personal question.

Anything

> You said something bad happened to you? It's why you don't like having your picture taken?

Yeah

> Was that true?

That part was true, yeah

> What happened?

If I answer you'll think I'm crazy

You might already think that, after tonight

It might be why you don't want my picture anymore

> I want that.

> I want that a lot, actually.

I think you're a little crazy, if I'm being honest.

> Because of the story I told you with my brother?

Because you're stalking that woman

What woman?

I know where you're going with this, Sam

You want to talk about my life because you're comparing it to the life of the Genevieve that you've been stalking

I don't know what you're talking about.

But you do

Sam

Mon amour

We don't lie to each other, remember?

I thought maybe she was you.

That's because I gave you her last name

I had to learn what life was like in Paris somehow

She visits the Seine, you ask me how I'm doing, I tell you how much I enjoyed the Seine today. Pretty convincing, huh?

I'm surprised you didn't catch on sooner honestly

Because I told you I never post photos of myself

And she does

> I thought maybe you were just shy.

And tonight even though I've confessed

You're still looking at her

You still want to believe she's the woman that's been talking to you

> I'm just trying to make sense of things.

No

She's the one

She's the woman you've been picturing all this time

I get it

She's pretty

> I'm sure you're pretty too

> Do you want to know the truth of it?

>> Of course.

> I am

> Pretty

> I'm stunning

>> I believe it.

> But now you're afraid to see, aren't you?

> When you said before you knew I was pretty and you could tell, it was because you thought you'd been stealing glimpses of me this whole time

> Wasn't it?

>> I'm sorry.

>> I didn't think it would hurt.

> That's okay

> I forgive you

> I happen to know I'm your type

We've seen each other before

Ginny, I'm going to ask you something and I promise not to be mad. But I want you to be honest.

Always

Are you playing a trick on me?

A trick?

Like I did, with my brother. When I locked him in the shed.

How would I be doing that?

That's not an answer.

Yes, and no.

Please explain.

It's not a trick, because it's real

But it's similar. Because I like that you're scared

I'm so curious to see if you'll scream

> Will you tell me when we saw each other?

You remember

You're thinking of the right redhead now

> No.

I'll give you a hint

I was wearing this dress

Cream silk

> No.

Are you screaming, Sam?

> I don't understand.

No

You wouldn't

> You wanted to know the worst thing I'd ever done on purpose.

Yes

> Because you already knew the worst thing I'd ever done on accident.

I knew the worst thing you ever FAILED to do.

> It was you.

Do you want to hear about the bad thing that happened?

Why I don't get my picture taken anymore?

Why I'm vulnerable?

> Yes.

You know the end

Let me tell you the rest

> Please

I was 22

I was seeing this guy

He was a real asshole

He hit me

> Once

> It wasn't fun

> I never minded pain. I was a real tomboy when I was younger, so scrapes and bruises and broken bones were all fine

> And the tattoos obviously

> I'd been in fights and brawls and gotten my face busted up a couple times at concerts

> But I was never going to let a man hit me

But he did.

> He did. Once, like I said

> You see on TV and stuff how women stay after that, but I didn't

> We were fighting and he hit me and I told him to pack his shit and get out of my apartment

Did he?

> No

> He grabbed me and bent me over the counter

>> Did he…?

> Take me?

> No

> There wasn't any time for that

>> No time?

> It was like

> I think when he hit me, he thought I was so in love with him that I was gonna take it

> But I didn't

> So he thought for a second he was going to make me

> Like if he could make me do what he wanted I was going to let him stay and keep hitting me like he wanted

> But I fought him there, too.

> I stepped on his foot, and I kicked out and I elbowed him, I think?

> It all happened really fast

> But what I hadn't seen, because he had my face staring at the counter, was that he'd already grabbed the knife

> So when I made him stagger back and I turned around

> Well

He stabbed you?

> Yeah

> The first time he looked as surprised as I was

> It was all shock at first

> There wasn't even any pain I was just so stunned that he'd stabbed me

> And he pulled the knife out of me

> And do you wanna know the funny part?

What?

> He apologized

> He fucking apologized to me

He stood his ground about hitting me and he'd JUST been trying to force himself on me, but stabbing me was like, where the line was

THAT was too far

That's not that funny.

No

I guess not

I laugh about it sometimes though

He looked more scared than I was, and he said sorry and then he put the knife right back in

And still sometimes I look back and I think about how stupid he looked standing there

Apologizing

I'm sorry that happened to you.

Yeah

Me too

But, if it hadn't, you know

> We wouldn't have met

No.

I don't suppose we would have.

What happened next?

> You know what happened next

Tell me.

> Well he left the knife in me that second time and I took it out
>
> Lotta blood when you do that, you know
>
> It got all over the nightgown I was wearing, got over everything
>
> I slashed him up real bad
>
> Didn't kill him
>
> But he was real fucking baby about it
>
> He swore and staggered back and tried to get his shirt off so he could press it up against the wound
>
> And I ran

> Out into the street.

Yep

> In the rain.

Yeah

You can finish the story from here if you want

> I don't know that I want to.

I want you to

Tell me

What's the worst thing you ever did?

> I watched a woman die in the street.

While you were in Seattle?

> On a business trip.

Why didn't you help me?

> Honestly?

> We don't lie to each other, mon amour. We're past that now

> You were so damn beautiful.

> I was all turned around and I found that dead end and was just about to leave. You staggered around the corner and right into my arms.

> I thought you'd help me

> I should have.

> I meant to.

> The truth is I fantasized about it while it was happening, and a couple nights after. I thought maybe I could play the white knight and you'd be desperate to thank me and we'd fall in love.

> But you didn't do that

> No. I didn't.

> Were you scared?

> A little.

> You were a beautiful woman, half naked in the rain, bleeding all over me. And you were so far gone. I didn't want to risk taking the fall for whatever had happened to you.

You wanted to be seen as good

So Mommy would keep tucking you in

> The thought struck me.

> It made me hesitate for just a second too long.

> Want to know something funny… that isn't all that funny?

Always

> I almost got caught anyway.

How?

> I couldn't leave you.

> I'd always wondered what it would have been like if my brother had actually died because of me. If I could have lived with myself. It was different with you, obviously, because you were a stranger. But it answered the question.

Could you have lived with it?

> Yes.

> There was something I liked about it, even.

> I never felt close to my brother after what happened. But I felt close to you.

I was a stranger

> It didn't feel that way when I watched the light leave your eyes, mon amour. I've never experienced that level of intimacy with… anyone.

> Not until tonight.

Was it worth it?

> Yes.

> I want to say no.

> But you're right, we're past lying to each other.

> If I had saved you, we wouldn't be having this conversation now.

> Even if you had thanked me and loved me, we wouldn't be talking like this.

> I'd have never seen such a fear in you, and you never would have inspired it in me. No one has ever toyed with me like this.

You're probably right

But we'll never know

> So.

> Will you tell me the trick, now?

The trick?

> How they found you?

Who found me?

> The paramedics. The good Samaritans and doctors and whoever brought you back from the brink of death?

No one brought me back

> So what? You're a ghost?

Is that so hard to believe?

> Yes.

> Sorry. Yes, it is.

I never believed in ghosts either

> Let's say I believe you…

You should. I died in your arms.

> Why not haunt me? Why not throw things around and mess up the apartment and drive me to the brink of insanity? It seems like an odd revenge, getting me off every night for a year just to confess.

You haven't figured it out yet?

> No.

I can't hurt you, Sam. I can manipulate the lights a little, and switch TV channels, and mostly, I've gotten good at working your phone.

> Still. Ominous text messages. Veiled threats. Why the dating site scam? Why the sexting and the dirty talk and the leading me along for a year? Why not hurt me?

What hurts more than love?

Sam?

Mon amour?

> Can I still get that picture?

Of course

I keep my promises

Do you keep yours?

> Of course.

Prove it

> I've forgiven you.

> I've done everything you asked.

> And you were right.

> I loved you.

You promised you'd always love me

> I do.

I need you to do something for me

Something I can't do myself

> You want me to kill him?

> The man that did this to you?

> Give me his name, and I swear I will go to him.

> I'll make him suffer for what he did.

Don't think I've forgotten him

He's on my list next

> Next?

I'm building up to him

I had to get this practice somewhere

So I was just… what?

A test run?

No

Don't think of it like that

You were a…

A what?

You were an experience I didn't get to have while I was alive

What do you mean?

Love?

You love me too, don't you?

Does it matter?

Yes

No?

I don't know that I can love, mon amour

We had fun

And I meant it when I said I loved the person I was when I was trying to keep you on the line

It felt right

We felt right.

We did

You gave me back a little piece of what your cowardice robbed me of

And it's why I forgave you

I meant that part too

I DO forgive you

I'm not angry anymore

Then why are you doing this?

We can make this work.

MON AMOUR

> It can stay like this and nothing has to change.

But I need the rest of what you owe me

I don't want to watch you grow old

And my other killer walk free

And I don't want to be trapped here in the internet as you shrivel up and lose your mind

> I'm not ready to go.

Neither was I

> I don't think I'm brave enough.

It's just like going to sleep

And I'll be right here with you until the end

> Promise?

I promise

> Say the whole thing

I promise I'll stay with you until the end

Je t'aime toujour.

Yes.

Je t'aime toujour, mon amour.

There you go

That's not so bad, is it?

Just a little deeper

Good

Now

Remember why this is happening

Remember why you're doing this

[IMG (opened)]

Acknowledgements

So much of the credit for this book goes to the brilliant Ruth Anna Evans.

She is one of the most amazing cover designers I've ever met and she gets better every single day. I have a number of her covers that I have stories written for, but for years I've gotten tripped up on anything past the drafting phase.

When I was in my last writing dry spell I pitched the concept of her doing a prompt cover for me that I would take, title and all. She delivered the art for *Mon Amour* that evening with my name already on it, at an absolute steal of a price. It is, in every sense, a Cat Voleur cover. It's got a pretty lady on it, the colors are gorgeous, there are splashes of red, and of course, it's a little French.

I wrote the rough draft of the story that night and for the longest time didn't know what to do with it. It felt too special to put in a collection of other stuff where the cover art wouldn't get used, and I strongly felt like it was too short to release as a book. Ruth Anna, again, encouraged me in every conceivable way to just go ahead and release it as a stand alone. In the magical world of self publishing there aren't as many constraints. In trying to learn about the process, *Mon Amour* is my way of finally embracing that.

If I want to release a teeny tiny little chapbook that's American French and all text messages, I'll have a hellish time formatting it, but nobody is going to stop me. Thank you for that very important lesson, Ruth Anna.

Content Warnings

While there are no depictions of the following featured in this book, the topics of assault, abuse, attempted rape, child death and grooming are all mentioned briefly in passing. There's also sexting, profanity, and strongly implied suicide/self-harm.

Please read responsibly.

Also By

Revenge Arc

All of These People Are Going to Die 4: Heck House

Puppet Shark: The Novelization

Kill Your Darlings

The Desert Island Game

Made in United States
North Haven, CT
02 April 2024